Digging for Dinos

Read more Haggis and Tank adventures!

Digging for Dinos

by **Jessica Young**
illustrated by **James Burks**

SCHOLASTIC INC.

For Steve, who digs fossils -JY

For Mike, Dan, and Renee, my fellow picture-book paleontologists -JB

Copyright © 2016 by Jessica Young
Illustrations copyright © 2016 by James Burks

All rights reserved. Published by Scholastic Inc.
Publishers since 1920. SCHOLASTIC, BRANCHES, and associated logos are trademarks and/or registered trademarks of Scholastic Inc.

Library of Congress Cataloging-in-Publication Data included below:
Young, Jessica (Jessica E.), author.
Digging for dinos / by Jessica Young ; illustrated by James Burks.
pages cm. — (Haggis and Tank unleashed ; 2)
Summary: Haggis, the Scottie, and Tank, the Great Dane, two dogs with active imaginations, set out to search their neighborhood for dinosaurs to play with.
ISBN 0-545-81888-9 (pbk. : alk. paper) — ISBN 0-545-81889-6 (hardcover : alk. paper) — ISBN 0-545-81971-7 (ebook) — ISBN 0-545-81972-5 (eba ebook) 1. Great Dane—Juvenile fiction. 2. Scottish terrier—Juvenile fiction. 3. Dinosaurs—Juvenile fiction. 4. Imagination—Juvenile fiction. [1. Great Dane—Fiction. 2. Scottish terrier—Fiction. 3. Dogs—Fiction. 4. Dinosaurs—Fiction. 5. Imagination–Fiction.] I. Burks, James (James R.), illustrator. II. Title.
PZ7.Y8657Di 2016
[E]—dc23
2015011356

ISBN 978-0-545-81889-6 (hardcover) / ISBN 978-0-545-81888-9 (paperback)

10 9 8 7 6 5 4 3 2 1   16 17 18 19 20

Printed in China   38
First edition, March 2016
Edited by Katie Carella
Book design by Cheung Tai

TABLE OF CONTENTS

CHAPTER ONE
DINO DAZE

Haggis woke up early and got ready for the day.

He clipped his toenails.

He snipped his mustache.

He polished his dog tag until it sparkled.

Tank did not have time for grooming.
She was busy reading.

Tank spotted something sticking up out of the ground. She ran to check it out.

4

Tank dug for dinosaur bones.

All she found was a stinky old
tennis ball.

While Haggis brushed himself off, Tank read some more.

Do you think there are any real, live dinosaurs still around from dino days?

I think <u>you're</u> in a dino daze. Dinosaurs are extinct. There aren't any left.

There aren't any <u>left</u>?

Right.

There aren't any <u>right</u>?

No, there aren't any <u>left</u>.

9

Haggis did not want adventure. But Tank used her best begging skills.

Finally, Haggis gave in.

Haggis and Tank got ready for a dino hunt!

CHAPTER TWO

BACK-TRACKING

Haggis and Tank set out in search of dinosaurs.

13

They hadn't gone far when Tank found some tracks.

Haggis and Tank followed the tracks.

Soon there were more tracks.

Haggis was getting worried.

Tank was getting hungry.

Haggis and Tank kept following
the tracks. But they didn't see any
dinosaurs.

Tank put her paw in the print.

Tank saw another print.

Just then, there was a rustling in the trees.

Haggis did not want to find out what it was.

CHAPTER THREE
EGG-SITTERS

Haggis and Tank ran through the forest.

They hadn't gone far before Haggis needed a rest.

Haggis rested.

Tank took a look just around the bend.

She found a surprise.

A dinosaur egg!

But where is your mama?

Poor, little, lonely egg!

Tank looked at the egg. She had an idea.

Haggis looked at the egg.

Tank sat on the egg.

Then Haggis spotted another egg.

Tank, look!

Egg-cellent! Twins!

We'll need another egg-sitter.

You want <u>me</u> to sit on it?

Just think—you could be the first dog to hatch a dinosaur! You'll be famous!

Haggis sat on the egg.

Haggis and Tank sat . . .

and sat . . .

and sat.

Then they saw <u>another</u> egg in the ferns.

Haggis and Tank played musical eggs.

They started out fast.

But soon they were dragging their paws.

Haggis and Tank built a nest.

They each picked up an egg and tucked it in.

Two down and one to go! Soon they'll be all snuggly.

Tank went to get more leaves.

Haggis went to get the last egg.

D-d-d-dinosaur!

Yes, a baby dinosaur! We should start thinking of names. Let's see, there's Emma, Pablo, Darwin—

T-T-T-TANK! D-D-D-DINOSAUR!

Tank turned around.

She saw a triceratops.

SNO-O-O-ORT!

The triceratops did not look happy.

CHAPTER FOUR
DINO-S'MORES

The triceratops stomped toward the nest.

39

Haggis tripped.

The egg went flying.

Tank dove for the egg.

She missed.

But the triceratops caught it.

The triceratops put the egg in the nest.
She covered the nest with leaves.

Tank waved good-bye. The triceratops wagged her tail.

Tank threw the bone.

The triceratops was not so good at playing fetch. But she was great at baseball.

She rocked at ringtoss.

She was a super sword-fighter.

And she was the perfect partner for Tank's circus act.

The new friends built a fort.

Then it was snack time.

Haggis and Tank and the triceratops roasted marshmallows. Tank stuffed them between dog biscuits and added some cheese.

The triceratops was tired.

ZZZZZZZZZZ . . .
ZZZZZZZZZZ . . .

Looks like it's nap time.

Listen—
dino-snores!

Soon Tank was sleeping, too. But Haggis couldn't nap with all the noise.

The noise got louder . . .

and louder.

Then Haggis heard a new noise.

CHAPTER FIVE
FUNNY FEELING

Tank woke up just in time.

ROAR!

Suddenly, a giant T-rex came crashing through the trees.

CRASH!

ROAR!

The drooling dino towered over them.

Haggis and Tank thought they were goners.

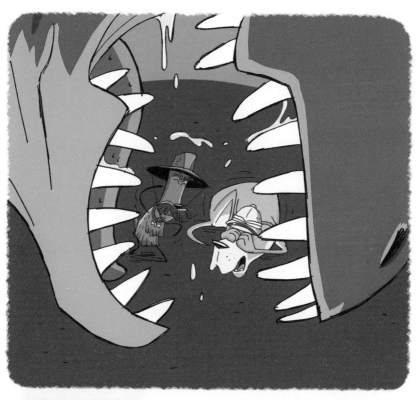

RUMBLE!
RUMBLE!

But the T-rex ran off.

RUMBLE!
RUMBLE!

Or maybe he was running _from_ something!

CHAPTER SIX
LUCKY DOGS

Haggis and Tank ran fast.

But the lava was faster.

They came to a cliff. There was nowhere to go.

Haggis and Tank feared the end was near.

They prepared for the worst.

Haggis and Tank were happy to be home.

Jessica Young

grew up in Ontario, Canada. She has never gone on a dino dig, but she is always up for an adventure — real or imaginary. Jessica loves playing with words and dreaming up stories! Her other books include SPY GUY THE NOT-SO-SECRET AGENT, the FINLEY FLOWERS series, and the award-winning MY BLUE IS HAPPY. HAGGIS AND TANK UNLEASHED is her first early chapter book series.

James Burks

lives in sunny California. Even though he is not a dog, James enjoys chasing squirrels, getting belly rubs, and running around the dog park. His other books include the award-winning GABBY AND GATOR, BEEP AND BAH, and the BIRD AND SQUIRREL graphic novel series.

How much do you know about Digging for Dinos?

Look at the pictures and words on pages 18 and 19. What is happening?

Why do Haggis and Tank play "musical eggs"?

Look back at page 49. What is the difference between <u>ate</u> and <u>eight</u>?

Why is the lava freezing when it touches Haggis and Tank?

Choose a dinosaur. Draw pictures and write words to describe a game it might be good at based on its physical appearance.